OTHERWISE
ALONE

Cover Design: Mayhem Cover Creations

Interior Formatting: Mayhem Cover Creations

Editing : Tamara

DEDICATION

For everyone out there who has read my writing in the past and offered me their continued encouragement to get out there and actually publish something, it is to you my first real publication is dedicated.

I would never have gone this far without all of you!

And for Tamara, who has been there through every step of this crazy *being a writer* journey for a long, long time.

TABLE OF CONTENTS

Preface   I

Chapter One | Meaningless Existence   3

Chapter Two | Resolved Tension   17

Chapter Three | Sowed Seeds   35

Chapter Four | Accepted Fate   49

Acknowledgments   55

Excerpt From Otherwise Occupied   57

Other Shay Savage Titles   79

About the Author | Shay Savage   81

PREFACE

Evan Arden

In blazing heat and almost complete isolation, I hide in the Arizona desert and wait for the day my boss tells me I can come back home. My only companions are my Barrett rifle and a Great Pyrenees named Odin.

I check my email regularly – it's my only link to what has become the outside world. Everything in it reminds me of what is currently out of my reach, and I wonder if I will end up rotting here after all.

Maybe it isn't exile.

Maybe it is an execution.

The days are long and the nights are longer, until a young woman suddenly appears on my doorstep. I'm all for getting a little – it's been ages – but she makes me long for more.

CHAPTER ONE
Meaningless Existence

It's fucking hot.

Even though I'm naked, I've kicked all the blankets off in the middle of the night.

The sun isn't even up yet, and it's still blisteringly hot in the middle of the desert, somewhere west of Pinon, Arizona. I roll over on my back and try to blow air down my chest, letting the sweat there mix with my breath to cool me down a bit. It helps, but only when I'm actually exhaling.

The bed squeaks as I drop my legs to the side and hope I don't end up with another fucking splinter from the ancient wood floors. My eyes fall to my Barrett, a long barreled rifle with an elaborate scope, which is propped up in the corner of the room, next to the bed. It is my constant reminder of how I ended up here. I stretch and moan a little before I take a quick piss and dig around for a clean pair of boxer shorts, my jeans, and a faded *Jesus and Mary Chain* concert T-shirt. Once I'm dressed, I go outside and check the level of gasoline I still have for the generator. If I don't run a

3

fan and only use the electricity for cooking and checking my email, I've got enough to keep me going another week or so.

Internally I hope that will be enough, but I know in the back of my head that it probably won't be. I will have to make the one-hundred mile trek to a gas station where I have yet to be seen. Lots of people pass through the area on the highway several miles from here, but they don't ever stop twice in the same place. Even if they did, chances are no one would notice, but I'm not one to take chances.

Before I can head back through the door of the small, two room house, I hear a magnificent sneeze followed by the thumping of four canine feet across the dusty ground.

"Come 'ere, Odin," I say with a yawn, and the Great Pyrenees lopes over to get his head scratched. Though his white coat is still pretty close to his skin, in this heat he needs another haircut. I wonder if I have enough juice to charge up the electric trimmers. If there isn't, I'm going to have to do it by hand with a pair of scissors. Odin isn't going to like it much, and it will probably end up looking like shit, but it's better than overheating.

I fill his water dish from the pump outside and wipe my forehead with the back of my hand. There's just enough light to see by as it streaks across the barren landscape while the sun decides to make an appearance. I do a quick look around, check the wires hooked up to the battery of the old Chevy truck in the back of the house, and verify they're still connected. The wire runs the perimeter of the two acre property and would set off the vehicle's horn if breached.

It's not the best security around, but I'm supposed to be dead anyway.

I stretch out, do a few pushups and sit ups, then jog around the shack a few times before I head back in. Odin follows me back inside, and I take quick inventory of the place out of habit, not because I don't know what I will find. There isn't much to go over – a bathroom with rusted out fixtures, a kitchen area with a mini-fridge full of room temperature – that is, warm – bottles of water, and a small electric stove. The main room is mostly occupied by my twin-sized bed with a cast-iron frame, once painted white, but is now chipped and falling apart. Pushed against the wall is a card table with two folding chairs. There isn't even room for a full sized chest of drawers or anything, so the small amount of clothing I do have is folded up in the drawer of a short nightstand. I showed up here with a single duffle bag, so I don't have that much, anyway.

"Fucking paradise," I grunt to myself.

Odin looks up at me and snuffs. He hardly ever barks but seems content to huff through his nose and occasionally whine at me. I'm not one to talk to the dog a lot either, though he is my steadfast companion. He's eight years old, and I've had him since half way through his first year. I don't know why I decided to walk into the county animal shelter that day, but he was with me when I left, and he's been by my side just about constantly since then.

After making myself a peanut butter sandwich, I pull one of the warm bottles of water out of the fridge and drink it down. I stretch again, rub Odin's wooly head, and grab the rifle before I go out to the front porch to sit in the rocking chair and watch.

It's not like I really think I'm going to be found at this point – I've been out here in this Godforsaken place for a quarter of a year – but I don't have much of anything else to do, and I can't leave until I get the go-ahead to do so. *Watching* at least gives me the feeling that I am doing *something* because I find it difficult to do nothing at all. I wish I could read, but I tend to get very lost in a good book, and that would drop my defenses to a completely unacceptable level.

Just because I *haven't* been found doesn't mean I *won't* be. I know this from experience.

I pick up one of Odin's rubber bones from the corner of the porch and toss it out into the dust. He stands and looks out at it, wags his tail a few times, and then drops back down at my feet.

"You used to want to play fetch, you lazy thing."

Another huff through his nose is all I get in return. I'm fairly certain what he means to say is it's too damn hot for that shit. I sit and tap the run-down front porch with the toe of my boot as I rock back and forth with the sniper rifle across my lap and Odin at my feet. The heat continues to be oppressive, but there is at least the hint of a breeze in the air today. It's still unbearable, but it's a slightly better version of unbearable than it was yesterday. It's a hell of a lot better than a bunker in the Middle East even without the breeze.

Lunchtime.

I fire up the generator and the stove to boil some water, add part of a box of pasta to the pot, and heat up some sauce. I let the fan run while I eat because the afternoon is just too fucking hot and I need a little temporary relief. The pasta is nicely al dente, but the sauce comes out of a jar and sucks. I remember homemade sauces from Rinaldo's kitchen – his wife slapping my hand away as I tried to get a taste before dinner was on the table.

While I eat, I fire up the netbook PC and wait for it to acquire enough of a satellite signal to download my email. Odin watches for cues from me, but when he gets none he just drops at my feet with his head on his front paws. The fan shuffles the hair on his head around, and he huffs again before closing his eyes for a bit of a nap.

The electronic beep tells me my email has loaded. There is one message from Pizza Hut, offering me my choice of any pizza with any topping for ten bucks – fucking tease that email is – and three additional, similar advertisements. I have also apparently won the Swiss Lotto four times, can obtain Canadian prescriptions for Viagra at a discount, and the President of a country I have never heard of wants to give me one-point-two million dollars from his off-shore account.

Nothing from Rinaldo.

I don't delete the messages – I just shut the PC back down again.

I wash the dishes, put them in the cupboard, turn off the fan and the generator, and then drop back into the rocking chair on the porch. Odin wakes up and follows. He lets out a big yawn, stretches, turns himself in a circle, and then settles back down at my feet. I reach out and rub the back of his neck with the toe of my boot.

My eyes scan the horizon.

Sage brush, packed red earth, and dust devils.

I lean my head back and close my eyes for a moment. Visions of a cool, rainy alleyway and the sound of gunshots fill my head. I can see my own arm upraised and the barrel of my Beretta turned on its side as a man in a dark blue suit runs away from me. My arm jerks twice, and he falls.

"What the fuck, Arden? He wasn't the target!"

"He was a witness."

"But shit...Rinaldo's not going to be happy about this."

"I've done worse."

Well, I thought I had.

Apparently killing the nephew or cousin or some such shit of Greco's mistress pissed the guy off. Since Greco's group was

Rinaldo Moretti's competition, the potential for an all-out mafia war was pretty high, which is why I had to disappear. Greco didn't know who did it, but he was determined to find out, and it was better if I was just not around to be found. Rinaldo was ticked, and there had been a moment there in the first fifteen minutes of his stalking around in his office when I thought he was going to put a bullet in my brain, but he didn't. Exile was the next best alternative. That was just after Memorial Day weekend, and tomorrow will be the first of September.

I open my eyes again and stare at one of the dust devils as it spins and jerks around for a minute before dissipating into the dry ground. I roll my shoulders one at a time and glance down at Odin, wondering how he can sleep while wearing a fur coat in this heat. I scan the horizon again, rather haphazardly.

Movement.

I am instantly alert.

This is not a dust devil or a dry, tumbling shrub. The movement is on the dirt road leading up to the small house and it is definitely human. Whoever it is, he or she is too far away to been seen clearly without a little ocular assistance. The rifle comes to my shoulder reflexively. With my left eye closed, my right eye looks down the scope, focusing on the target some three-quarters of a mile away. Through the crosshairs, I can see the figure much more clearly.

It's a girl.

What the fuck?

A woman, I suppose – maybe twenty years old. She's walking sideways just a little, like she's not really looking where she's going, and stumbling every once in a while. She's not carrying anything, but as she approaches I can see there is a small backpack strapped to her back. It's not big enough for any real supplies, but more like one of those things the college girls wear for a purse — something that is certainly more decorative than useful.

As she comes closer, I get a better view and learn a little about her. She's been walking for maybe an hour or two at most because she's not showing any signs of dehydration and she doesn't appear to have any water with her. Her shoes are very dusty, though, so it's not like she just started walking, either. Her hair is pulled up on top of her head, but I'm pretty sure she's only done that recently. It's haphazard and definitely not done with the aid of a mirror. She was either in a rush when she put it up, or it was done as she walked to cool off her neck.

She's a freaking klutz, tripping about every forty steps over nothing but her own shoes, as far as I can tell. For some reason, that makes me smile a little. I shift the weapon and scan the horizon behind her from left to right, but there's no one else to be seen. I consider my options.

Option one - shoot her. I really don't want or need any company, and company in general is a risk. Pros — I don't have to think about it anymore, and it's generally safer for me. Cons — she's just some innocent chick whose car probably broke down, and killing her is kind of a shitty thing to do.

Next option — let her walk right on up here. If she was from Rinaldo, I'd have some notice about it, and if she was from Greco's organization she wouldn't be approaching the house tripping over the dust with nothing on her but a little bitty backpack. Pros — I wouldn't have to dig a big ass hole in the dry, packed ground. Cons — I will probably have to talk to her.

She stumbles again — just a little. It is barely noticeable if you aren't really paying attention, but I am. I always pay attention. She's maybe five-foot-four and a hundred and twenty pounds. Her tennis shoes are covered with a pretty thick layer of dust, and as I lower the scope a little I can see a slightly clearer spot on the edge of her left shoe – near the laces. She must have tried to wipe it off, but it's been some time ago and it's all dirty again. I re-estimate and decide she's been walking for at least two hours, and she's got something serious on her mind – at least serious to *her*. As she walks she is completely oblivious to everything around her.

Either it is really that important, or she is really that ignorant. A few hours in this heat is not a good thing. I try to come up with any other alternatives, but I don't think of many. She's obviously not Native American, so she probably doesn't have family too close.

Odin's head pops up, and he growls low as he looks out towards the young woman.

"You're a little late," I tell him, and he huffs at me. I focus the scope back on my visitor, and my finger hovers over the trigger for a moment, but only a moment. I have no problem shooting a woman – done it plenty of times before – but she is just lost, and that doesn't seem like a decent reason to die.

I lay the rifle back across my lap. She's close enough to watch without it now, though she still hasn't even looked up from the dirt road. If I am quiet enough, I'm pretty sure she'll run right into the house.

She trips again, right at the perimeter of the property, and the truck's horn starts blaring. Awakened from her trance, her head jerks up and she falters in her steps as her eyes take in the shack, the Chevy, and then me as I stand up, rifle still in hand and pointed in her general direction.

Odin immediately stands alongside me with hackles raised and starts to growl loudly. He doesn't take it any further because he can tell I'm not particularly alarmed. Wary, yes – because I'm not stupid – but I'm not overly concerned, either. Even if she started running, it would take a track star at least a minute to reach me, so I stand up from my chair, walk over to the truck, and disconnect the alarm so the horn stops.

I walk back towards the porch but stick to the dirt instead of going up the steps. I don't need the extra height to keep her closely in my sights, and I figure since I'm obviously not shooting her just yet, I am probably going to end up talking to her.

Odin is walking in a figure eight pattern in front of me, watching the girl's approach. I snap my fingers near my hip, and he walks around behind me. He sits on the ground and looks up to me expectantly.

Her approach slows as she gets near me. She almost seems to hunch down a little, as if there would be some advantage to making herself invisible at this point. Her eyes are trained to the rifle in my grip as she takes a final step forward, stops, and opens her mouth.

"Um...hi!" she calls out. Her eyes dart around, showing her nervousness. Her hand comes up in a short wave, but it's not too convincing a gesture.

I look her up and down, reassessing now that she is closer. My conclusions are all the same – she's lost, been walking for about two hours, and she came from the south. The closest road in the south is Highway 264, so she is definitely going in the wrong direction. She has another twenty-five miles before she hits another road. If she wasn't standing in front of me right now, she'd probably be dead before nightfall.

"Do you want to die?" I ask her. My tone is probably a little harsher than needed, but the question just had to be asked.

Her eyes go wide, and she takes a step back from the barrel of the rifle. I resist the urge to snicker as I gesture out towards the open desert with the dangerous end.

"Not the very best area to look for a picnic spot."

She glances around the barren landscape, then at the weapon in my hands as it points back towards her head. She laughs nervously and wraps her fingers around themselves in front of her stomach. Her top teeth pop out and bite into her lower lip as her face turns to a grimace, and she stares hard at the ground for a while. When she looks up at me, I can see her throat bob before she speaks again.

"My car broke down," she says softly. Her eyes drop from mine, and she looks off towards the dirt road for a second. The muscles in her right hand tighten a little, making her fingers jerk in response.

There is no doubt in my mind she is lying.

"Did it now?" I reply softly.

"Yeah, overheated, I suppose," she says with a little more conviction. "I thought I was heading back the direction I came from, but obviously I wasn't."

"Want to get some water, and I'll drive you back to it? I'm sure I can take care of a little radiator trouble."

"Oh!" Her eyes go wide, and her feet begin to shuffle.

That's right, baby, I'm not buying your shit.

"You don't have to do that." She reaches up and fiddles with the poof made by the hair band at the top of her head. "Maybe I could just use your phone? My cell can't get any reception, and I think it's dead now anyway."

"I don't have one," I reply.

"Oh." Her eyes drop back to the ground.

I keep looking at her, but she won't meet my gaze. I debate calling her out on it directly or letting her dig herself deeper. It doesn't really matter one way or another, so the decision is based completely on my own desire to see what she says.

"You want to tell me the real reason you're wandering around out here?"

Her teeth take that moment to bite right into her lip again, and I wonder if she's going to make herself bleed.

"That obvious, huh?"

"Pretty much."

"My mom always said not to join any secret societies because I was the worst liar in the world."

I don't reply because there's no reason to respond to that. I just wait and watch. She's looking at the ground and seems to have become suddenly lost in her own mind, likely in nostalgia about her mom or some other aspect of her childhood. When she doesn't say anything after a minute, I switch the rifle from one arm to the other and her eyes widen.

At least I have her attention again.

"I had a bit of an…an *argument*…with my driver," she finally mumbles. "I was dropped off in the middle of nowhere."

It's the truth, but not all of it. I figure it's all I'm going to get, and since I really don't care, I decide to move on from this conversation.

"Want some water?" I ask. I move the rifle up to my shoulder, pointing the end at the sky.

"Yes, please." Her relief is obvious, but she is also understandably cautious in her movements. She follows me tentatively to the door and stands just outside of it. Odin sniffs around at her feet, and she pats his head. He seems undecided about her, likely reflecting my own feelings.

"It's not particularly cold," I tell her as I pull a bottle out of what would be a refrigerator if it was turned on, "but it *is* wet."

"That's perfect, really," she says.

I walk near the door and hold the bottle of water just out of her reach. I'm curious about how she will respond. Will she step inside the spider's parlor to get the water she needs to survive? Or will her own fears and paranoia make her stay on the rickety porch and refuse to take the risk?

It takes her several seconds until she realizes I'm not going to move, and she slowly takes two steps forward. Our fingers brush against each other's as she takes the bottle from my hand. There's a tinge of red on the tops of her cheeks which wasn't there before. She's embarrassed, but about what? Is it because she's taking water from a stranger or because she's admitting to needing help?

Or maybe it's because our fingers touched and she realizes she's alone with some guy she doesn't know.

I want to laugh at the idea, but I manage to contain myself.

"Thank you," she says and then clears her throat. She twists open the bottle and tips it up to her lips. She starts to drink way too quickly, and I immediately grab it from her, causing her to startle.

"Not so fast," I say, "or you'll make yourself sick. Sip it."

I place the bottle back in her hand, and she nods slowly at me. She takes a small sip, pauses, and then takes another. I return her nod, convinced she isn't going to make herself puke on my floor now.

"What's your name?" she asks.

"Evan," I tell her.

"I'm Lia," she says with a smile. I'm not sure if it is due to her continued nervousness or if she really just wants to be polite. I watch her closely but don't respond. "Um...Lia Antonio."

Italian. Figures. I should have known from her features. She doesn't have any accent, though, so she's not first gen or anything.

I keep staring at her. I know it's making her nervous, but I'm not one for small talk and I don't want her to get the impression that she's going to stay here and gossip away the evening with me. I consider picking the rifle back up and making it clear she needs to be on her way.

On her way where?

If I kick her out, she's dead before the sun sets. What am I supposed to do – offer her a fucking ride somewhere? I don't even know – or care – where she's going. I'm also supposed to stay right where I am except when I need to go somewhere for supplies.

Getting low on gasoline, I remind myself.

Fuck.

I push the thought from my head. I don't want to have to spend at least a couple hours in a truck with some chick I don't know. She's an idiot for even being here.

I reconsider almost immediately. She *is* an idiot, but that is for getting herself in the situation at all, not because she is here now. She doesn't have a choice at this point. Going back out into the desert is suicide.

"Hungry?" I hear myself ask, and I want to slam my head into the wall.

"Um…a little, but really – you don't have to go to any trouble."

"Well," I say, "it's my dinner time, so I'm going to cook. If you want something, speak up now."

She steps from one foot to the other a couple of times as she stares at the wood slats that make up the floor.

"I guess," she finally answers. "I mean, if you are making something already, that would be wonderful."

Too fucking polite.

CHAPTER TWO

Resolved Tension

We sit at the table, and I serve up what I managed to scrounge for dinner. It's a better meal than I would have made for myself – definitely. Fried potatoes with peppers and onions mixed in with it, along with canned peaches and a couple bottles of water. It still isn't much, but the way she tears into it tells me how hungry she really is.

I leave the generator going, and the fan points close to us so we can at least be a little more comfortable while eating. Odin plops himself down next to the fan to reap the benefits as well. He watches Lia pretty closely but backs away when she reaches out her hand. When she asks me if he's friendly to strangers, I can only shrug. He really hasn't been around too many people. It's always been just the two of us.

"This is really good," Lia says as she takes another bite of the potatoes. "Where did you learn to cook?"

"Camping," I tell her. It is close enough to accurate. "We did a lot of hiking in the middle of nowhere, so I can make a meal out of most anything as long as I have a fire to cook it."

"We?" she pushes. "You and your family?"

I hesitate before shaking my head.

"I don't have one."

"I'm sorry," she says quietly as she bows her head. I wonder if she thinks they're all dead and she's saying a little prayer for them or something. I decide to take the moment to get a little distance.

"I'm going outside for a few," I tell her. I need to hook the alarm back up to the truck, which means first running out to the point where she tripped it up and set it off. "I'll be right back."

Not sure why I feel the need to tell her that.

"It's getting dark," she says softly as she looks out the window.

I don't reply because it's such an obvious observation. Will she tell me I'm tall next? After picking up my rifle, I head out and Odin follows at my heels. He sniffs the ground as he keeps pace with my jog. Once I reach the general area, I follow her footprints in the dry ground until I come to the thin, detached wire and twist the metal part of it back together.

Odin and I run back to the truck and clip the whole thing to the truck's battery. I walk slowly around the house using the scope on the horizon but see nothing of interest. I refill Odin's water dish, feed him, and head inside again. I leave the front door open, which I do most nights. It doesn't have an actual lock on it anyway, and it works particularly well this evening since the fan is on and it creates a nice cross-breeze.

Lia is still sitting in the same spot, tearing the label from her water bottle. I look her over, wondering what's going through her head. I can make a lot of logical guesses, but there are still too many parameters. She could be thinking of her mother, the asshole who ditched her, or what she is going to do now.

"I assume you are staying here tonight," I say. I don't know if I'm answering the question she is pondering or not, but it still has to be something on her mind. Besides, I feel resigned to letting her stay.

"Oh, no, no," she says with a shake of her head. "I couldn't impose…"

I want to laugh, but she probably wouldn't appreciate the humor. I go with straightforward instead.

"There really aren't a lot of options," I point out to her. "It's late. I'm tired and going to bed. You can stay or you can go, whatever you want obviously, but I wouldn't go anywhere until tomorrow."

"I guess you're right," she admits. Her fingers twist around each other on top of the table.

I stand slowly and start collecting the dishes and fill the sink up with water.

"Oh!" she suddenly cries out. "Let me do that!"

She's beside me a second later, apparently planning on washing the dishes herself. I consider for a moment, and then take a step back.

"By all means." I'm curious to see if she really intends to do it or if she is just trying to be polite. Her hands go into the sudsy water, and she begins to scrub. There aren't many, and she's done quickly and efficiently. When she places the last dish in the drying rack, I realize I've been watching her the entire time.

Slowly, I pull the towel from my shoulder and hand it over to her. She mumbles a thank you as she takes it and quickly dries her hands. She looks around the tiny kitchen area and finds the little loop used to hold towels and threads the drying cloth through it before looking back to me.

For a long moment, I only look at her and try to figure her out. Some things are obvious – she's running from someone. Maybe he dumped her on the side of the road and maybe she ran off, but she's trying to get away from him. That much is clear. On impulse, I check out her ring finger. No ring, but there's a clear mark around the skin – she's worn one until recently.

Interesting.

Is it lying in the dust out there in the road or hidden away in a little pocket of the backpack she left lying next to the still open front door? I tilt my head to one side and feel the brush of the fan's wind against my neck. I need to turn it – and the generator – off for the night. I do both before walking to the far side of the little room where I live.

It's still too fucking hot.

Gripping the hem of my shirt, I pull it up over my head and off before tossing it into a basket under the window. I reach down and thumb open the button on my faded blue jeans. I feel my mouth turn up into a half smile as Lia blushes and looks away from me – as if there is anywhere else to really look in the shack. I shake my head and try not to laugh out loud as I dump my jeans around my ankles, bend over to pick them up, and fold them a couple of times before placing them in the nightstand drawer.

Deciding to at least leave my boxers on for her sake, I drop down to the bed and toss the thin sheet back just in case she wants to use it. It is way too warm for a blanket, even a thin one, but who knows? Maybe she is one of those who always needs a blanket.

"Um…where should I sleep?" she asks quietly, and I can't help but chuckle.

"There's only one place to sleep," I say, which should have been pretty fucking obvious. Rolling and scooting to my side to offer her as much room as possible, I gesture to the other side of the twin bed. "Right here."

She looks around a bit, and I can almost hear her mind contemplating her options. There are the rocking chairs on the porch and the card table in the kitchen, which wouldn't hold half her weight. Other than that, there is the wood floor to sleep on – that's it.

I shake my head slowly.

"Just lay down."

I watch her throat bob as she swallows again, then walks slowly over to the side of my bed. She doesn't bother taking anything off, which doesn't surprise me at all. She'll be way too hot to sleep, but that's her problem.

Actually, she's just plain hot.

I'm pretty sure it's not just because I haven't seen an actual female for three months that makes me think like this. Her hair is gorgeous and makes me want to run my fingers through it while my cock slides in and out of her mouth. She's got a perfect build, too. She's not too skinny, which I fucking hate, but has kind of an athletic build. She isn't quite muscular enough to remind me of the chicks who served with me, but still well-formed. She's got a real woman's hips, which I want to grip while I pound into her pussy. Nice ass, too, which makes me want to roll her over on her stomach and grasp both cheeks while my cock pistons in and out of her backdoor.

There seems to be a theme to my thoughts.

She bites down on her lower lip as she first sits on the bed and then stretches out next to me, which is when it occurs to me that I'd really like to just kiss her, too. I chuckle silently to myself and try to get in the most comfortable position possible. I lie down on my side still facing her and lay my arm across my own body with my hand resting on my thigh so she has enough room to lie down without having to touch me. She also lies down facing me, which I find intriguing. A lot of people would have turned around and faced away from a relative stranger, feeling protected by their own backs. She knows better and realizes she needs to be able to see me so she's not taken off guard.

She's also staring at my bare chest.

Her eyes are just a little wider than I would expect from someone contemplating sleep, and her muscles are tight and stiff. She's not mentally tired at all, but only going through the motions because it's time to go to sleep, not because she wants to. She may be physically exhausted, but her mind won't let her relax. She's too anxious to sleep, and I wonder if her thoughts are more on the strange man whose bed she is in or the one who dumped her on the side of the road without regard for her safety.

That thought pisses me off a bit.

I watch her watch me, and every time I look at her lips I think of either covering them with my own or maybe filling her mouth with my cock. Every time I look lower, I want to find some other warm place to hide my dick for an hour or so.

Yeah, there is definitely a theme.

"You're making me nervous," she says.

I glance up from her hip back to her face.

"How?" I ask, though I'm pretty sure I know the answer.

"You keep staring at me."

I try to hold back a laugh, but I can't help myself.

"You are by far the most interesting thing I have had to look at in a long, long time."

Her eyes are wary and nervous, and I feel a little bad. My flippant comment probably isn't going to help her get any sleep, and that really isn't my intent. I decide to lay it all on the line for her.

"Look..." I start, but then I pause. I'm not sure how to say what I want to say without scaring her, and I don't want to scare her. I want to fuck her, but I don't want to scare her. If I play all of this right – if I read her perfectly – then I just might get the chance. I can't fuck it up though. If I misread her in any way, I will say or do the wrong thing, and she will just become more agitated. I want to have her quietly moaning my name into the pillow as I come in her, not freaking out on me because I pushed in the exact wrong way.

I finally decide on the direct approach.

"You don't have to be scared of me. If I was going to hurt you, I would have already. If I was going to kill you, you'd be dead. If I was planning on raping you, you'd be raped, okay?"

I hear her sharp intake of breath.

Okay, maybe that was a little too direct.

She tenses at my last sentence, which doesn't surprise me. Most chicks are more fearful of being raped than being killed. Something about her posture and expression seem off to me, though. As I look her over I realize that though I have shocked her a bit, she's thinking about it in a slightly different way. It's not pure fear, as would be the obvious reaction.

I think about this for a minute and start watching her a little more closely. It does seem to make her...*react*. Her chest is rising and falling a little faster, her eyes are dilated, and there's a bit of a tinge to her cheeks that wasn't there before. I'm not sure nervous is the right word – anxious seems more like it. Maybe even something slightly different. Like maybe she's thinking about what it would be like, and not in a completely bad way.

I've seen chicks get raped - usually right in front of their dad or husband or whatever as a means of punishing him for whatever he fucked up. That shit just goes with the territory in my line of business. I don't participate – I'm just a killer, not a torturer. That's an art form I don't care to learn. My skills are all with the guns, and the closest I ever see my victims is through the scope. With rape, the chick gets damaged, and I know no woman really wants that. That's not the same as thinking about it, though, and I know the difference between fantasy and reality.

I process the information in my head.

Some guy, one who is close to her and maybe even her husband, dumped her on the side of the road…and now she wouldn't mind a little consensual, rough sex.

Interesting.

It's temping, but the more I think about it, the more I decide I'm not going to act on it. I'm not sure my cock is in agreement because it's threatening to rear up and be noticed. In a bed this size and with our close proximity, I really doubt it will be overlooked, so I close my eyes for a minute, breathe deep, and think about a few head shots until I'm in control again.

Well, I am until I open my eyes and see that she is still staring at my chest. Every minute or so her gaze drops down over my abs and maybe even a bit lower as well. The tip of her tongue slips out and moistens her lips right before she takes air deeply into her lungs.

I feel the slight vibration in the mattress as she shudders a little. For a moment, I think it's fear, but her eyes show something else. She wants me. She's thinking about running her hands over my chest, and the thought is making me hard. My mouth acts on the thought without really having a deep consultation about it with my brain first.

"Touch me," I say.

Her eyes widen as her tongue darts out over her lips again. "What?"

I hate that. People do it all the time, and I know it's "human nature" or some such shit, but I hate it when people use the "oh I didn't hear you" excuse to give themselves time to think about how they want to answer you. That is exactly what she is doing, and I'm not going to give her the chance to think.

"Touch me," I repeat as I nod towards her hand. "You want to – go ahead."

She hesitates, and her chest rises and falls with her deepening breaths. Her eyes move to mine, back down to my chest, and then back to my face again. I can almost see her mind working behind her eyes – weighing the options and trying to decide if she is going to go for the gusto or not. She wants to, but she's afraid of the consequences.

"Take the chance," I say softly.

Her eyes are on mine again, and I know she's made her decision. She licks her lips once more before slowly reaching out with one hand. My skin can't help but twitch as her feathery light touch connects with my abs. I'm a little surprised because I thought she'd touch my chest first, and the sensation on my stomach is unexpected. It's also too damn close to my dick, which is now being very obvious just a couple of inches below her fingers.

Hoping she will agree that it's only fair, my hand moves slowly from my own leg over to her waist. I lay it right on top of the hem of her shirt – just above the curve of her hip – and just let it sit there a moment. Her eyes dart up to mine, and I can see her throat bob a little as she swallows nervously.

She looks back down to where her hand touches my skin, and her tongue runs over her lower lip. With a light touch, her hand moves up to my chest and slowly traces the outlines of the muscles there. She finds her way to my shoulder before going back down to my stomach again. My hand grips her slightly on her waist. It's only reflexive, but she looks up at me anyway.

She doesn't meet my eyes, though – she is focused a little lower. Her lips purse slightly, and I can see the increased speed of her breaths in the way her chest rises and falls. I want to place my hand on her chest to feel her heart rate, but I hold back.

For now.

"Kiss me." My voice sounds raspy to me, like my throat is dry and full of sand. I watch her eyes get wide for a moment, flickering quickly between my eyes and my mouth. As much as I want to lean forward and just take her mouth with mine, I stop myself from doing so. Letting her take the lead – at least for now – is important.

Soon, though…soon I'll be in control. Once she's decided she really wants it, I'm fucking taking over because that's what she really needs.

"Go on," I say with my eyes locked on hers. "You want to."

"I do?"

"Yes."

"And how do you know that?" Her tone is somewhat defiant but not enough. She might not want to want it, but she does.

"I'm a very good judge of character," I inform her.

"You are, huh?" She cocks her head to one side and looks up at me. Her eyes are dilated even more now, and I know she's just trying to think her way out of it.

"Stop stalling." My fingers grip her side a little to pull her minutely closer. Just a touch of encouragement, which seems to be all she needs.

My eyes stay on her as she moves slightly closer. She hesitates one last second before her lips tentatively touch mine. I'm not having any of that, though. She's opened the door, and it might as well be a pair of those gigantic wooden double-doors that grace the front of some huge Bavarian castle because I'm coming in.

I grab the back of her head with my hand and pull her to me, opening my mouth and finding her tongue with my own. She groans against my lips, and I tilt my head to one side to get a better angle. She tastes sweet, like the peaches we had with our dinner, and I want to devour her.

There is nothing soft or gentle about what I do. I want her, and I can sense the desire inside of her. She's not looking for a brief make-out session. Whatever happened with whomever she was with pushed her to this. She wants to be fucked, and I am happy to oblige. My hands grab at her, and my fingers dig into her flesh a little.

My tongue dances with hers.

Maybe more like a mosh pit than dancing, but *whatever*.

I slide my hand down her back and pull her body flush against mine. My cock is peeking out between the opening of my boxers, and I grind against her stomach. I need to get her shirt off of her as quickly as possible. And her jeans. And everything else.

I need to be inside of her. Mouth, pussy, ass – I don't care. I just need to merge with her…blend…be one…

She turns her head to break the kiss and to take a breath. I don't bother to stop, but instead move from her lips to her chin and then lower. Her head tilts back as I move down her neck, letting my tongue flick out over her heated skin. I get to the hollow of her throat before I am met with the cloth of her shirt, which pisses me off. I want her tits in my mouth, and I'm tired of playing around. I grasp her fingers and push her hand down until it's resting on top of my rigid cock.

"You want this?" I whisper in her ear, my hot breath making her shiver. I push against the back of her hand and tilt my hips at the same time, basically smashing her hand against my dick. "You say the word, and I'm going to give it to you just how you need it."

Her eyes are wide, and I know she wants it, but I still wait. *She* needs to know it, not just me. Her wide eyes finally look up to mine, and I feel her fingers twitch against my cock. She nods slightly, but it isn't good enough.

"I want to hear it," I say to her. "Tell me you want it."

"I want it." No hesitation.

I don't need further encouragement.

I grab both of her wrists and hold them together in my hand, raising them high above her head and pushing them into the pillow. My lips smash down on hers, and my tongue invades her mouth. She gasps and cries out into my mouth, but I don't stop. I don't even slow down.

I need this as much as she does.

My free hand moves to my boxers and pushes them down enough to free my hard and expectant cock before I start moving with purpose. I grab the end of her shirt then and pull it up until her bra is exposed. I straddle her, my mouth still locked to hers, and rub my dick against the skin of her bare stomach. I reach down, hoping she's wearing a bra that clasps in the front, but she's not, so I tear the fucking thing off of her.

She groans in protest this time, struggling against my grip on her hands. I move back enough to release her lips.

"What the hell are you doing?" she cries.

"I'm going to tear your clothes off and fuck you so hard you won't walk right for a week," I respond. "You want me to stop?"

Her eyes dilate further, her chest rises and falls rapidly, and her mouth opens and closes a couple of times before she shakes her head emphatically. I don't need verbal confirmation this time, and I yank her shorts part way down her legs instead. Her panties come with them, and I don't bother getting them all the way off because my fingers can already reach what my cock is looking to find.

The tips of my fingers slide over her outer labia very lightly – teasingly. Her hips push up, trying to find the friction, but I don't give it to her. I just lightly touch her at first until she is squirming under me. The tip of my index finger glances over her clit before seeking her opening and pushing inside.

She gasps at the sensation, but she's wet enough. It's not because it's uncomfortable at all, and is probably more in anticipation of what my cock is going to feel like. She's still moving around a lot, though her hands are still pinned. I lean over her and run my tongue around her nipple, and she moans.

Then I bite her.

Not hard – not enough to hurt, but definitely enough to notice. Her body tries to rise off the bed, but it doesn't work – she's trapped under me, and it's making me seriously hard. I add another finger, slide in and out of her a couple more times, then pull them out and use the moisture to coat my dick.

"You ready for this?" I ask huskily as I position myself at her entrance. "I don't have any condoms, and I'm fucking you bareback. I'll pull out if you want."

"I'm...I'm on the pill," she says, breathless.

"It's a good thing," I reply, and I shove into her.

The noise she makes is nearly a scream, and for a brief moment I think I have crossed a line. I release her hands, and she immediately grabs my head and pulls my mouth to hers. I feel an instant of relief before I kiss her roughly and use my now freed hand to wrap around her tit and pull at the nipple. However, most of my focus is on the warm, seriously tight channel where I've just placed my cock.

Holy shit.

It's been a while – a long while – and it feels fucking fantastic.

I rock my hips into her quickly – pulling out to the tip before slamming back home. Her body jerks each time I hit her center, which tightens her up and squeezes my cock. I'm only slightly aware of her tongue in my mouth because my cock feels too glorious.

I thrust into her harder, and she throws her head back and breaks our kiss. She groans loudly, and I take the opportunity to lean back a bit and grab both her hips in my hands.

"You better hang on, babe."

She makes a little noise in her throat that almost sounds like a squeak, but she obeys – gripping my forearms with her hands and wrapping her ankles around my calves. The bed squeaks as we progress, and I move rhythmically as my cock claims her pussy. Each push is fast and deep – almost violent as I bottom out in her, buried balls-deep with every thrust. I pound her and pound her until there is sweat running down my back and into my eyes from my hairline.

I run my hands up her sides and focus on her tits. I love the way they feel in my hands – perfectly round globes of soft skin and pebbled nipples. I pull at them, and I want to suck on them more, but I like the pace I've set fucking into her and I'd have to slow down to reach her with my mouth. Even touching them slows me down, and I want to pound her harder. More importantly, I want a decent view of her ass.

I pull out, and she whimpers under me as I get up on my knees and wrench her hands from my arms.

"Get on your hands and knees," I tell her. "Spread those legs."

My voice is quiet, but my tone still makes the words an order. She complies immediately, and I hear her whimper a little as I move up on my knees and into position between her legs. I grab her hips and slam my cock back inside of her. Her ass is fabulous, and I dig my fingers into the soft flesh as I move.

She's fucking tight this way, and every time I slam up into her, she gasps and her pussy tightens up. I close my eyes for a moment, tilt my head back, and focus on the feeling of her wrapped around my dick as I fuck deep into her. When my eyes open again, I look down to where my cock is sliding in and out of her for a minute, but the sight is too fucking awesome and I can't keep looking or I'm going to blow. Instead, I lean over her back and slide my hands up her sides and around to grip her tits. I pull at her nipples – not hard at all, but enough to give her a little more stimulation. She moans and tries to turn her head around to see me.

I take one hand and place it on the back of her neck. With just a little pressure, I guide her head to the pillow and wait for her to turn her face to one side before I lean in with a little more weight, holding her there. I keep slamming into her as my other hand moves south, finds her trembling stomach, and then her pulsating clit.

I bring her to the brink, back off a bit, and then bring her to the brink again. She is crying out, sweating, and practically shaking. My own legs are threatening to give out, so I push her down flat with my body. I lay on top of her back, my legs just inside of hers.

My hand is sandwiched between her pussy and the mattress, and I continue to run my finger around her clit. I have to adjust my position a little, but a few moments later I'm slamming into her again – not as deep, because the angle isn't right for deep penetration – but just as hard as before.

My hand releases her neck, and I grab her hair instead.

"My cock feels so good fucking you," I growl into her ear. "You like that? Huh?"

A groan is the only response I get, but it is enough.

I slam into her harder, hold myself deep inside for a moment, and then slowly slide almost all the way out. I would have pulled all the way out, but it would be too awkward to get back inside of her without getting her back up on her knees again, and I like having her all splayed out under me the way she is.

She likes it, too.

"Do you know how easy it would be," I moan, and my voice is gravely and husky in her ear, "to fuck you in the ass from this position?"

I feel her tense, and there are goose bumps springing up over her neck and shoulders. I smile slightly – she's never taken a cock up the ass before. My lips press against the skin below her ear.

"Not this time," I whisper, and I feel her relax underneath me for a brief moment. My finger circles her clit again, and she cries out. Her body clamps down on my cock, and I push into her with a snarl. My thrusts are shallow but quick. I keep rhythm with my finger on her clit as I pound into her as hard as I physically can. Her cries come in time with the creak of the bed as I slam into her.

I can feel it coming – the tightness in my thighs and the squeezing sensation in my balls just before the wave cascades over me, leaving me grunting and holding my breath. I come hard and deep inside of her, arching my back a little to push in as far as I can. As the wave subsides, I drop onto her back and my breaths come in short, hot pants against the skin between her shoulder blades.

I stay there for a while, just listening to the sound of our breathing and waiting for my body to relax. My hand is caught between Lia and the mattress and is starting to go a bit numb. I like where I am though and don't really want to change the position much. I settle for a slight roll to my side, pulling her body tight against mine until we're in a classic spooning position.

Evan Arden – hit man gone spooner.

I almost laugh out loud.

Lia's heart is still pounding as I hold her against my chest. She turns her head over her shoulder a little and looks me in the eye.

"That was…incredible," she says through panting breaths.

I chuckle.

"I know."

She laughs out loud.

"What do you mean, *you know*?"

I stare at her intently, silently debating just how straightforward I want to be with a woman who literally stumbled into my life barely a few hours ago. If I tell her, it will reveal quite a bit about me – an aspect I tend to keep to myself – to an almost perfect stranger.

A stranger who just had his cock inside her…

Well…yes.

Still, there are people I have known for years who don't know about how much detail my mind seems to pick up and categorize in a short amount of time. *Deductive reasoning*, Mother Superior had called it. She even made me read Arthur Conan Doyle books.

Eventually I used it against her to get emancipated at the age of sixteen, and she was nearly ousted from the church altogether.

I realize Lia is still watching me and waiting for an answer, and I decide to throw a little caution to the wind.

"You like getting fucked hard," I say with a small shrug.

"How do you know that?" she asks quietly.

"What? Aside from the massive orgasm you had?"

"Yes," she replies, her voice still soft. "I mean, how did you know before? Before you...um...started?"

I shut my eyes for a moment and try not to sigh too loudly.

"You really want to hear this?"

She hesitates but answers in the affirmative.

Who am I to argue?

"Aside from the obvious bullshit nature of the story you gave me when you got here," I start, "the ring finger of your left hand still has the indent of a ring you wore for a long time – either engagement or wedding – whatever it was. You were too tight to have been having sex regularly, which means even though you were still wearing your ring recently, you weren't getting it on with your fiancé or husband. You're a little timid, which means he was abusive to you – maybe not physically because I don't see any evidence of that – but at least mentally or emotionally. Guys that are shits to their women tend to feel bad about it, so when he tried to make up for whatever shit he did to you, he'd make slow love to you as a way of apology. You probably grew to associate that kind of sex with the shitty apologies he never really meant, so as sweet as he wanted it to be, it left you feeling emotionally empty inside. That's why all you want now is to be fucked."

I open my eyes and look into her shocked expression.

"Hard," I add.

CHAPTER THREE

Sowed Seeds

Lia's breath comes in quick, short pants as she drops back down on my chest. With one arm wrapped around her back and my softening cock still buried inside of her, I gently run my hand over the top of her head before kissing the same spot.

I'm exhausted, and I feel fantastic.

I haven't fucked the same chick twice in a row since college, and never in the same night. At three in the morning, we are on the fourth round. It is like my cock couldn't get enough of her pussy and her luscious ass. I still haven't fucked it, but that's okay, too. Maybe in the morning...

I wrap my other arm around her shoulders and hold her close to me. I close my eyes and slow down my breathing – trying to match hers as our heartbeats seem to flow into one. Her head rests under my chin, and her hair tickles my neck.

I like it, and it brings deep, restful sleep.

I wake, feeling the difference in our positions immediately. I've shifted lower in my sleep, and instead of holding her against my chest, my head is cradled against her body. One of her arms is around my shoulders, and the other is slowly stroking through my hair. It's still fucking hot, and if I try to move I will likely find our skin stuck together.

And I really, really don't give a shit.

Of the times I have woken up with a woman in my bed – and I can probably count those on one hand – I have never woken up quite like this. It's unsettling, but when I turn my head to look up into her eyes, the next set of feelings that course through me are far more unsettling.

She smiles at me, and it feels like I've been turned inside out.

She is unusually beautiful. Not text-book, air-brushed, model beautiful, natural and clear and...*lovingly* beautiful. It's as if I have just looked into the face of the mother of God, and my Catholic days are far, far behind me. It is more than that, though. My muscles relax into her, and I feel safe. I feel comforted. I feel strangely *submissive* to her – like there isn't anything within my power I wouldn't do for her.

"Hi," she says. The sound is quiet and unassuming.

I want to respond in kind. I want to be nonchalant. I want to ignore the churning of my guts inside of me as she looks down at me.

"Hey," I finally sputter. Her hand keeps running through my hair, and I almost want to shake my leg the way Odin does when I hit the exact right spot.

Get a hold of yourself, Arden.

I close my eyes briefly and take a deep breath. It doesn't help at all because now her scent is all around me. It smells like me and her and sex all mixed up together, and I want to make good use of my morning wood.

"You okay?" she asks, and I nod reflexively.

"Just need to pee," I tell her.

When I push up and away from her, our skin makes a ridiculous sound as it separates. She giggles, and I make the mistake of looking at her again.

I smile down at her, afraid to open my mouth, and then turn quickly to the little toilet in the corner. There's no door – only a shower curtain attached to the door frame, which I don't even bother to pull around as I relieve myself. I grab my toothbrush for a quick once-over before I head back to bed.

She slips out of the bed when I'm done and heads for the bathroom area as well, first blushing and asking if she can borrow a toothbrush. I watch her ass as she walks away from me, and my fingers tense up a bit, wanting to grab a hold of it again.

I'm not done with her.

As soon as she gets close to the bed, I'm on her again. I sit up and pull her into my lap, grabbing both her ankles and wrapping them around my hips. Holding tight to her waist, I raise her up over my cock and lower her onto me. She rises up on her knees and moves slowly over me a few times, but it's not enough, and I can't see her ass.

I really like her ass.

Pushing her up and off of me, I position myself on my back as Lia straddles me. I shake my head at her.

"Turn around," I say. "Face away from me. I want to see your ass while you ride me."

She blushes. My cock is glistening with her juices, and she's blushing at me. *Holy shit*, why do I find that so hot? She slowly lifts her leg over my hips and settles her knee down on the mattress. She shifts and moves down a little until she's in the right spot, and I grip the base of my cock to help guide it back inside of her. She groans as she lowers herself, and after she's adjusted to the position, I grab her hips and pull her down onto me.

Tilting my hips upward each time I pull her down onto me makes for maximum depth, and I feel practically high, though I've never smoked weed in my life. I imagine this is what it might feel like as she slides up and down my cock, faster and faster as she moans and tosses back her head.

I let go of one hip long enough to grab one of her hands and hold it in front of her, down by her clit.

"Touch yourself," I order. "Make yourself come on me."

The sight of her back and ass as she rides me and brings herself to orgasm is one of the most beautiful things I have ever seen in my life. Not that I've really seen a lot of beautiful stuff because my life hasn't led towards that kind of shit, but she is truly phenomenal. The curves on her…the way her hair moves…the tiny droplet of sweat cascading between her shoulder blades…

I growl and cry out as I push inside once more, holding her hips against me as I fill her. My head drops to the mattress as I angle my hips a couple more times to milk the feeling a bit. I sit up and wrap my arms around her, letting her fall back against my chest as I roll us to our sides, almost dropping us both off the small bed in the process.

She giggles through her rapid breaths, and the motion makes my softening cock fall out of her. She twists around to face me, and I push the hair from her forehead.

"What do you do for a living?" she suddenly asks as she props herself up on one elbow with her head resting on her hand.

"I'm retired military," I respond automatically. It's the truth, easily validated. I roll onto my back and try to catch my breath as she begins to pepper me with questions, and I continue to answer in the vaguest way possible.

"That explains a lot," she mumbles under her breath as her fingers trace over my bicep. "I like your muscles."

"The better to hold you down and fuck you with, my dear."

She laughs as I roll over her and take her nipple between my teeth. I nibble, but only lightly. Between last night's numerous escapades, the lack of sleep, and the earlier morning romp, my stamina hasn't quite returned yet. I prop myself up on my hands and lean in to kiss her a couple of times before I lay back on my side facing her.

Her hand runs over my bicep again, then down my arm. Her head cocks quizzically to one side as her fingers trace over the slight dip at my waist right before they creep around to my ass. She gives it a bit of a squeeze before looking up at me with humor in her eyes.

"I like this part best," she admits as she blushes.

Heh. Birds of a feather or whatever the fuck the saying is.

I grab her butt, too, and bring us closer together.

"I like this one better."

She giggles, blushes, and then stares at me again.

"What?" I ask.

"Nothing," she mumbles back.

"Tell me."

Lia hesitates before speaking again.

"Can I try something?"

I narrow my eyes and release her ass.

"Depends on what it is."

"Just...roll over a minute."

"Roll over?"

"On your stomach," Lia clarifies.

I glare at her a minute as she offers more encouragement. Finally I acquiesce and lay on my stomach in the center of the bed, watching her warily as she goes to the bag she has by the front door. I tense, watching her movements closely, and for the first time I feel agitated – sure for the briefest of moments I have been duped – she knows who I am and she's here to kill me. I am a second from jumping out of the bed and maybe wrestling her to the ground when she turns and holds up a small, round, shiny coin.

It's a quarter.

"What the fuck?" I ask. Lia giggles as she skips the fifteen feet back to the bed.

"I've always wanted to try this," she says. "You were in the military – it's just like the quarter test on the bed after you've made it up.

She *cannot* be serious.

"What, on my ass?" I ask incredulously.

"Exactly!" Lia giggles again.

I drop my head into my hands and close my eyes. I can't believe I'm submitting to this, but at the same time I cannot stop laughing.

"Flex!" she orders, and I comply.

I look over my shoulder and watch as she tosses a quarter at my backside…

…and misses the bed completely.

"Damnit!"

I'm laughing so hard my gut is starting to hurt, and I barely feel it when she smacks my ass and tells me to be still so she can try again. I try to hold in the chuckles, but she smacks me twice more before I'm still enough for her. This time it works, and I'm a little surprised myself when the quarter bounces off and rolls under the bed.

Lia jumps up and down, shouting and cheering. This makes her tits *and* her ass bounce around, too, so I flip back over and grab her, pull her back into the bed, and cover her mouth with mine.

"That's the dumbest thing I have ever heard of anyone doing," I mumble between laughs and kisses.

"It was awesome," she says. "I've always wanted to see that."

I want to fuck her again immediately, but now the laughing has worn me out, so I lay us both back down and just kiss her for a while longer. They are slow kisses, but they are just as hard and earnest as they were before. After a while, we are content to lay there and watch each other – breathless.

Eventually, Lia goes back to her questions.

"How old are you?"

"Twenty-six."

"Where were you born?"

"Ohio."

"Do you have any brothers or sisters?"

"Nope."

"How long have you been here?"

"A couple months."

"Are you going to stay?"

"Maybe."

She sighs and drops to her back beside me. I can feel her shoulder against mine.

"Evan, why are you here?"

Shit.

"Well, the atmosphere is awesome," I say, trying to pull off the joke and maybe change the subject as well. "The weather's never too cold, and I don't have to worry about any leash laws."

She looks at me for a long moment in silence. I turn my eyes away from her.

"You live in a rundown shack in the middle of nowhere," she says. "You have a laptop and a really freaky looking gun. You must have some money somewhere, so why would you choose to live here?"

"Well, you know," I say with a small, humorless chuckle, "if I tell you…"

I let my voice trail off.

"You'd have to kill me?"

I shrug. It is probably true, though for the first time in my life I actually have an opinion about it. I wouldn't really mind telling her and almost feel compelled to do so, but I know I can't.

"I was in the Marines," I finally speak quietly. "I trained in Virginia, was injured in the line of duty, and honorably discharged. Please don't ask me anything else."

Her fingertips cross my cheek gently.

"I won't," she promises. "I'm sorry."

I know I am giving her the wrong impression, but it is better than an outright lie, and I can't give her more details about my life afterwards. What would I say anyway? Oh, by the way, you just fucked an ex-Marine sniping expert turned hit man for a Chicago mob boss. Have a great morning.

Yeah…not likely.

Breakfast is quiet, and she joins me for a walk around the area with Odin after we're done. I want to ask her what exactly she plans to do today, but I find I'm a little anxious about her answer.

I don't want her to leave.

It makes sense, really. I haven't spoken to a single person since I drove to Pinon for gas over a month ago, and I only asked the sales clerk to confirm the price on a liter of Gatorade. Before that I hadn't said a word to a soul since leaving Chicago.

"It's temporary."

"What, until you find someone better than me and send them out to remove me more permanently? I'm not stupid, Rinaldo."

"So you claim, yet here you still stand."

"Fine. I'll go."

There's a touch against my arm, and her fingers slide from my elbow down to my hand. A second later our fingers are interlocked, and the sensation is both welcome and nerve-racking.

"Do you regret it?" Lia suddenly asks.

For a brief moment I think she can read my mind, but then I realize she's thinking about last night. Or this morning. Whatever.

"I'm a guy – we don't regret sex."

She snickers and shakes her head as she looks down to the ground in front of her feet. Her mouth immediately turns down, and she bites at her lip. I squeeze her fingers slightly, and she meets my eyes again.

"I don't regret it," I confirm, and she smiles genuinely.

"I've never done that before," she says softly. "I've never been that...*spontaneous*. You read me so well – better than he ever did."

"Does '*he*' have a name?"

She eyes me for a moment.

"William."

"*William* is an asshole," I say definitively. She smiles again, but the smile is a sad one.

"He wasn't always," she says. "When we were in school, he was so sweet and so different from the other guys. He grew up on the reservation near my hometown. He was...exotic, I guess. I think I also believed all that talk of alcoholism in Native Americans was bullshit."

"Just because it's a stereotype doesn't mean it never fits," I murmur.

"Very true." She nods her head. "My dad loved him, and I think when he passed away...my dad died of cancer two years ago..."

"Sorry," I mumble. I don't even know why I do it – I'm not one for standard responses.

"It's okay; it was a long time coming." She takes a deep breath before continuing. "My dad loved Will, and I know he wanted us to be together. I think...maybe I would have left him before it came to this if Dad hadn't loved him so much."

"You going to tell me what he did?"

"He drinks."

"You said that."

"Then he gets mean."

I wait for her to continue. I've already deduced most of this, though alcoholism would have been a guess only. There is nothing about her that points to his drinking as opposed to just him being a dick.

"He did slap me once," she says quietly. "I mean – it was a while ago – before we were engaged, so it's not like it would be out of character for him to do again."

She huffs out a humorless laugh. I found myself wishing the fucker would track her down so I could pick him off from a mile away.

"But even if he wasn't violent, he was never there. When he did come home, he'd yell at me all the time and tell me what a crappy job I was doing as a housewife."

Another laugh without heart.

"I was in school, so it's not like that was all I was doing. We weren't even married, just engaged. We've been engaged for almost four years."

"Why didn't you get married?" I ask. I feel her shoulders move up and down in a noncommittal gesture though I keep my eyes on the horizon. Odin is nosing around a creosote bush a few yards ahead of us.

"Lack of funds was always his reason," she says. "He always said he wanted to give me the perfect wedding even though that wasn't what I wanted. Dad was all for it though Mom was happy to have us stay as we were. Actually, she'll be thrilled to hear I'm not going back to him."

"You aren't?" I did not want to assume.

"Not this time," she says softly.

"What aren't you telling me?" I demand.

She bites into her lip before responding.

"When I told him to pull over, he did," she says. "He hadn't actually stopped yet when he reached over, opened my door, and shoved me out."

Lia goes silent, and I try to stop the feelings of rage inside of me. I haven't had such feelings in years, and it had taken years for me to get them under control in the first place. I want to find this asshole. I want to annihilate him. I want to tear him to fucking pieces to make sure he can never hurt her again. It would be easy and might even be a decent distraction from hanging around here. She just showed up yesterday – he can't be that far.

"I took a bunch of Aikido classes in college," she tells me. "I was always so...*ungraceful*. I thought it would help, but it never did. I did learn how to roll, though. That's what I did when I fell out, and I managed to end up on fairly soft ground."

The edge of her mouth twitches slightly, and the corners of her eyes clench, though it's barely noticeable. She still isn't telling me the complete truth, but I am fairly sure she's holding back some detail. Did she start the fight? Was he drunk while he was driving her? Why was he so angry?

Why do I give a shit?

I don't bother asking myself if I do care – it's so obvious there is no point in denying it to myself. I just can't figure out *why*. I haven't cared about anything since seven men and one woman trusted me with their lives and I failed them.

"I have to go to my mom's," Lia finally says. "She never really liked him in my life, and I know she'll be supportive, and I don't want her to worry. My cell doesn't seem to work anymore."

"It won't," I confirm. "Not anywhere near here."

"I figured."

"You can still call her," I suggest as I try to ignore the feeling in my chest when I think of her leaving. It's ridiculous and idiotic. "There's no landline here, but I can drive you into Pinon to call her."

"She'll still worry," Lia says with a shake of her head. "Will's probably called her by now, and God knows what he's told her."

"You want me to find him?" I say without thinking.

What the fuck, Arden? You going to kill this girl's ex?

She looks to me, and I don't miss her quick glance to the rifle. She is far too observant for her own good, and she knows what I mean as much as I do, even if it is a ridiculous notion.

"No," she says quietly, "I don't think that's really necessary."

I reach out and grab her fingers.

"Sorry," I mutter. "Reflex."

Oh great – that makes it sound so much better.

She actually flinches a little, and I might not have even noticed if I wasn't holding her hand.

"I won't do anything," I promise.

She nods.

"I would never hurt you," I add. It's so fucking important to me she knows I would never, ever do anything to hurt her, and I have no idea why.

She nods again.

"I know."

"Come back?" My fingers grip hers a little tighter. I want the words to sound like a demand, not a question. "After you see your mom, you can come back here."

I want it to be a statement…a charge…an order…but my own bizarre feelings of insecurity win out.

"You don't have to-"

"I want you to come back here," I interrupt. I need her to understand, even if I don't.

"Why?" Her voice is so soft, I can hardly hear her.

I don't know how to answer.

"Because," I finally say. I look into her eyes, hoping she'll find meaning there since my words are so inadequate.

Lia sighs and reaches up with her free hand to run it through my hair.

"How long will you be here?" she asks.

"I don't know. It could be days or weeks. I just don't know."

"I need at least a couple of days with my mom."

"Take them," I tell her. "Just come back when you're done."

She stares at me for some time without saying a word but finally nods her head. I don't know if it's meant for me or if it's just the way she is confirming her own decision to herself. I don't care – she's agreeing. Nothing else matters.

"All right, Evan," she says softly, "but only on one condition."

"Anything," I say. Again, all brains have left me.

"Tell me your full name."

"Lieutenant Evan Nathanial Arden." No brains whatsoever. Maybe the doctor who did my psyche evaluation and said I couldn't serve anymore was right.

Brains become completely irrelevant as she smiles at me again.

"Okay," Lia says with another smile. "I'll come back to you."

CHAPTER FOUR
Accepted Fate

Odin sits next to the open window of the truck, so I have Lia sandwiched between the two of us. I like it. I like it way too much, actually. Odin seems to have accepted her, or at least decided she smells enough like me now that it doesn't matter. He licks her hand when she pets him and even nuzzles her neck with his nose, making her laugh.

The journey is quiet, but I hold her hand in mine and place them both on her thigh. It is a two-hour drive to Tuba City, and the nearest bus station where she can get a ride the rest of the way to Phoenix. I want to take her to see her mother myself, but she makes it clear she wants to do this alone, and I know I can't really leave my station for the extended trip. At least I will be able to get some gas for the generator and some supplies.

I watch her legs as they move up the steps of the bus and wonder when they will be wrapped around my waist again. Lia turns back and gives me a smile that doesn't touch her eyes, and I return the sentiment. Then the doors close, and she is gone.

The drive back to the empty house is a blur – too uneventful to bother committing to memory. Even if it had been more exciting, my mind is too preoccupied to bother with it. Every thought points to her, and it's more than a little maddening.

When I walk in the door, I am followed closely by Odin, carrying his rubber bone in his mouth. He tries to engage me in play, but all I see is the empty bed with the sheets shoved down to the floor. I take a deep breath, hoping I can still find her scent in the house, but it's too faint, and I'm probably only imagining it.

Get your shit together, Arden.

I walk back outside and fire up the generator. Dinner is grilled cheese and half of a bag of salad I got from the store next to the bus station. I fire up the netbook PC as I munch on Romaine lettuce, cabbage, and carrot strips without any dressing. All they had in the little convenient store was the brand I hate, and there wasn't any Italian dressing at all. My email eventually loads as I'm on my second helping.

Pizza Hut – teasing me again. God, I would love a pizza right now.

I've won the Bank of Europe lottery. Is there a Bank of Europe?

Alienware would love to have me buy their new gaming machine.

And one more message.

Sender – Roger Moore.

Subject – none.

Body of message – come back.

The message was sent twenty-nine hours ago – I haven't checked messages since early yesterday. Roger – or rather, Rinaldo – would assume I had received the message and left by now.

I swallow hard and close the PC.

A thousand thoughts run through my mind, and I can't catalog them all into any semblance of order. I told her to come back, but when she gets here, the place is going to be empty. I can't hesitate to leave and head back to the city – I just can't. I have no phone number or any way to contact her. I didn't even consider it, and if she thought about it, she apparently didn't think it was necessary to give me her phone number.

Ride my cock for hours, yes, but not give me her fucking number…

Even if she had given me her number, I still don't have a phone to use in the first place. Not until I get back to Chicago, and there is no way I am going to ask her to come there. If I want to, I can have her found – there can't be that many Lia Antonio's with a mother living in Phoenix. I can certainly locate her mother at the very least, but then I wouldn't know what to say to her.

I'm trying to make excuses. I know what I'm doing and tell myself to cut that shit out. I don't lie to myself. It's pointless and destructive. I already know what I have decided because there really isn't any other choice. I'm not going to bring that girl into my life. No way in hell. The very notion is ridiculous, and I was probably just a little bit insane when I told her to come back here. It could never last.

There's a small duffle bag underneath the card table in the kitchen, which I haul out and deposit on the bed. My clothes go into it – the dirty and the clean. The netbook goes in there, too, as well as my spare pair of tennis shoes and Odin's bone. I reach over and grab the rifle, quickly dismantling it so it fits inside the duffel. I take a quick look around the place to make sure nothing important has been forgotten, and there they are.

Her panties – the ones I nearly tore off of her last night – wrapped up in the sheets on the bed. I reach over and untangle them, then place them deep inside the duffle bag.

I have to leave her something.

I briefly consider leaving her my boxers but shake that thought from my head quickly. Her little lacy underwear is seriously sexy – boxers are not. There really isn't anything I have I can leave for her, so I am stuck with the ultimately lame. I dig around in the "catch all" drawer of the kitchen until I find some paper and a pen. I sit in one of the folding chairs at the table and stare at the blank page.

What the hell can I even say?

I had to leave, but thanks for the great fuck?

I can't leave her my address. I don't have a phone number.

I can't tell her to come and find me in Chicago.

With shaking hands, I write a single word on the paper and then place it in the center of the bed.

SORRY

I take a step back, and a glint of silver catches my eye.

There is a quarter lying next to the pillow.

Reaching over slowly, I pick it up in my hand and hold it tightly, transferring the heat of my palm into the metal. My throat constricts, and I swallow past the lump before I open my fingers and let the coin drop next to the piece of paper.

Turning quickly, I grab a couple bottles of water for the road and head back out to the truck. I spend a moment dismantling the wires attached to the battery and rolling the wire up into a tight, round loop. I bend down to pick up the dog dish and a bag of kibble, throw them and the duffle into the back of the truck, and whistle. Odin appears from around the house, races towards me, and a few minutes later we are heading down the road.

As I steer the truck down the drive, it feels like someone reaches through my back and grabs hold of my heart, ripping it through my body and yanking it back to that tiny, hot little house. I keep swallowing, but it doesn't stop the burn in my throat.

Odin whines and noses at my arm. I look over at him and wonder what he sees when he looks at me. He noses my arm again, then licks my hand where it grips the steering wheel.

"Thanks, buddy," I say in monotone.

He whines again.

"I can't do that," I say softly. "I can't do that to her."

With my eyes staring toward the spanning horizon, I push thoughts of her from my mind, burying her memory in the darkest recesses of my brain. I wish I could have explained it to her – told her it was for her own good, but there was no way. Anything I said would either be a lie or too dangerous for her to know.

So I drive off.

Odin at my side.

But otherwise alone.

###

ACKNOWLEDGMENTS

Special thanks to everyone who helped pull this together: Chaya and Tamara for their marvelous editing, and Adam and Holly for the cover art.

I couldn't have gotten it done without all your help!

EXCERPT FROM

Otherwise Occupied

EVAN ARDEN TRILOGY BOOK #2

CHAPTER ONE
Hired Relief

It's fucking raining.

Again.

It wasn't that I minded the wet or the cold – I really didn't, but it screwed with my aim and I was still trying to get back into the boss man's good graces. I couldn't really afford to miss. Against my better judgment when it came to an easy escape, I had put myself a little closer than I liked to be for this sort of job. I had to be sure to be successful, and if it cost me my life...well, that was better than failure at this point.

With my left eye closed, I looked through the scope of my Barrett M82 rifle. The crosshairs focused on a set of double doors made of glass and metal. The doors led inside of a large office building, and there was a large "space available" sign over the entryway with a phone number to call if you wanted a thousand square feet, which was just right for your office needs. If you were to call the number, someone would answer, but you'd find there wasn't *really* any available space.

Not unless you had the right connections – preferably Russian, quite probably illegal Caspian Sea caviar, and definitely heroin. Those connections might get you a little corner office, but they would not, however, endear you to Rinaldo Moretti – my boss and sole owner of all the Moretti businesses. Some of those businesses were even legal.

Well, one of them was.

Sort of.

I shifted my hip and stretched my back a bit. I had been in the same position for a good seven hours, and I was hungry. I brought a couple of protein bars with me, but they were long gone. This job wasn't supposed to take this long, and I was getting frustrated and annoyed. I forced my breathing into a slow, regulated pace.

Frustration and annoyance were not my friends, not when I was on the job. I needed to keep my shit together long enough for my target to walk out the door and die.

Maybe the weather was causing a delay.

I reached up with my hand and tightened the cloth around my forehead. It was doing a decent job of keeping the rain from my eyes, but it wasn't helping with the whole comfort level. I didn't stop watching the door as I adjusted the bandana – never that. I had to be quick, efficient, and deadly.

No fuckups.

The last fuckup nearly cost me my life and had ended with me exiled to the desert for months, and that was just for killing the wrong guy. Missing the right one would be a lot worse. Of course, I couldn't hit or miss him if he didn't show up where he was supposed to be when he was supposed to be there.

"Calm, Arden." I blinked as I realized I was actually talking out loud to myself. Not good. I didn't like that shit, so I clenched my teeth a bit to remind myself not to do it again.

Everything had been perfect up until this point. After a week of scouring the Chicago city skyline, I had found the perfect building with the perfect view of the front doors. No visibility from the street directly below and nicely shielded from view of both the Willis Tower and the John Hancock Observatory. I only needed to be patient until...

...there he was.

I had no doubt the man in the grey trench coat was my target, though I had never met him before. I had studied his picture for hours yesterday to be sure I wouldn't make a mistake. I'd probably been through his family photos more often than his wife had.

I blinked once, placed the crosshairs in position, and smoothly pulled back on the trigger.

Only a muted thump could be heard as I sent the bullet down the barrel and into his left eye. Before he hit the ground, I was already back away from the ledge of the building and disassembling my rifle to shove it into a gym bag. I moved the clothes around inside to cushion the metal and make it undetectable from the outside of the bag and then headed swiftly to the rooftop entrance.

Three minutes later I was on the other side of the building, out the door, and then taking the stairs into the parking garage across the street. At the top of the garage was a gym where I held a membership, and I made my way to the locker room inside. With my bag padlocked into a locker, I hit the Nautilus equipment.

It felt good to work out a bit. I had been slacking.

All thoughts of Thomas Farmer, chief board member of Electro Industrial (now deceased), vanished from my head by the time I had done my third set of weights. If it sent the right message to others about which crime lord you should align with, I might get a bit of a break, and Moretti might put me back on my normal pay scale.

Probably not.

Sweat replaced the rainwater in my hair, and after I'd done a rotation on the Nautilus, I went for the treadmill. From the front counter, there was a chick there who kept giving me the eye. She even brought me a towel when I finally got off the machine. She'd done the same thing the last time I was here, but I didn't see her do it for anyone else.

"How was your workout, Evan?"

"Fine," I replied. "Thanks."

Great – she even bothered to look up my name.

She was twenty-four or twenty-five, five-foot-seven, blonde, and she had recently gotten a haircut – the ends were crisp and blunt – but she didn't like how it had turned out. She was trying to pull off a little ponytail for a hairstyle that was far too short, using a rubber band from around a newspaper. She didn't normally wear it that way, or she'd have one of those scrunchie things.

The first thought in my mind regarding her hair was to agree – it was too short. It also wasn't dark enough. She didn't have that classic Italian beauty look I preferred.

Preferred?

I wasn't actually aware I had a preference, and I considered this as I gave her a smile, a quick thanks, and then headed to the shower. While the water poured over me, images of long, smooth dark hair – almost black, but not quite – and matching dark eyes flooded my mental vision. I could almost feel her smooth skin against my palms.

I shook water from my head and quickly changed my thoughts.

I was probably going to have to change gyms even though I had only recently joined this one. I didn't need anyone paying attention to me, remembering me, and hitting on me. It was too bad, really, since the place was big enough to have a short wait time for the machines. Oh well. I could always work out at the gym adjoining my apartment, but the wait time for a treadmill meant spending half the day there for a sixty-minute workout.

Home again.

My apartment was a high-rise building right near the Chicago River. My boss owned the place, and it came with the job, so I didn't have to pay any rent or anything. It was a nice perk, though I would have preferred living in the country somewhere. I had never lived in the country, but I always thought I would like it – open spaces for target shooting and enough room for Odin to run around and chase squirrels and shit.

I nodded at Pete, the security guard, as I walked by. I had no idea what his last name was, but he was on Rinaldo's payroll. He smiled back at me, but the smile didn't reach his eyes like it usually did.

I glanced over him and quickly took in other changes. He was usually dressed pretty nicely, but on this day his normally ironed shirt was wrinkled, and the tie didn't match. His eyes were a little bloodshot from either lack of sleep or possibly actual crying – I couldn't really tell the difference.

It made me wonder if the wife had left him or if he left the wife, and then I decided it was probably the former. He had a kid, too – a young one not yet in school. I wondered if she found out about who he worked for and walked out. I wondered if I'd have to kill him.

Or her.

Maybe the kid.

Nah, probably not. Rinaldo was a businessman, and killing a kid rarely achieved anything that couldn't be achieved just as well by killing the parent.

The elevator dinged, and I pressed the button for the seventeenth floor. My apartment was the perfect location as far as I was concerned – right on the corner of the building, up high enough for my rifle to be very effective from a distance, and just two stories above the adjoining building. If I needed to get out via the balcony, I could. I usually took the elevator up and the stairs down but not for any particular reason. I was used to doing little things like that to keep myself in shape, and it was just a habit.

My eyes traveled over the door to my apartment, automatically looking for any signs of forced entry. There were none, but you couldn't be too careful. I slipped the key in the lock and opened the door.

"Hey, bud."

Odin jogged his way across the living room to greet me, and I rubbed his shaggy head. It was good to see his hair growing back in again – he looked better with it longer. Well, he at least looked more like a giant mop, a.k.a. a Great Pyrenees. When we had been out in the Arizona desert all that time, I had to keep it closely clipped to keep him cooled down. His buzz cut had been nearly as short as mine.

Maybe dogs did end up looking like their owners. Or was it the other way around?

Whatever it was, if dogs were man's best friend, Odin did his best to live up to the job. He had been with me for years and was about the only living thing around me I felt like I could actually count on. He would always be there when I got home from whatever I was doing. He never judged, never asked me a bunch of questions about why I was the way I was, and he never looked at me with fear.

He was my buddy, and it was one of the few things that scared me. I kept quiet about him because making it known I had something to care about – even a dog – was enough to bring those who had something against me out of the woodwork and into my private life. I didn't need that shit, and I couldn't always be around to protect Odin. As big and ferocious as he could look to some people, he was an easy target to others.

I started up my netbook computer before heading to the kitchen for some orange juice. It was the good stuff – fresh squeezed. I had been splurging on little things like that since returning to Chicago from the cabin in Arizona. The little things were so much more important than people realized when they had to go without.

Not that I had taken any of the small creature comforts for granted beforehand, either. It had been like that in the Iraqi desert, too, even at our base. Ration everything was the rule. It sucked, but it beat being left for dead in a hole.

Odin rubbed up against my leg, and I realized I had been lost in thought for a moment. I patted him in thanks and wondered for the hundredth time how he knew to do that. Like those service dogs that would get epileptics to lie down on the floor before a seizure starts to keep them from hurting themselves, Odin always seemed to know when I was thinking too much about the past.

He worked better than the drugs the doctors had prescribed.

I finished the OJ, took Odin out for a quick walk, and checked my email.

More lotto winnings.

Amazon would like me to review my purchase of a new set of headphones. I hadn't actually tried them out yet, but I'd be hanging out with Jonathan tomorrow and would probably need them. The dude smoked a lot of weed and usually started babbling when he was stoned.

A dating site called *Lost Connections* wanted to hook me up with an available woman in my area. I licked my lips and thought I was going to need a little company for the weekend but not from a fucking dating site.

Lost Connections.

Before I could stop it, expressive and soft brown eyes in the center of a heart-shaped face invaded my thoughts. Long, dark hair and a fucking luscious ass came next, but I pushed the rest of the memory away before it could really take hold and turned back to my email.

Pizza Hut had free cinnamon sticks with any large pizza.

"That's what I'm talking about," I muttered to myself. I clicked on the pizza link and quickly ordered a large stuffed crust with mushrooms and pineapple to be delivered.

Hey – it's what I like.

Fucking sue me.

When the pizza showed up, I sat down on the floor of the living room with my back against the couch and dug in, tossing bits of crust to Odin as I ate. It was a good thing I had gone to the gym today because I had eaten a shitload of pizza since returning to the city.

More thoughts about the simple things spun around in my head. Pizza, beer, coffee – even a gym where I could work out properly. For some reason, my pleasure at the thought of the mundane alarmed me. My tongue moistened my lips, and I grabbed the remote to find something to watch on the television.

I was definitely thinking too much. I had to stop.

Television wasn't a necessity; it was a luxury and a way to pass the time. I never really liked television much as a kid but found it was good for helping me relax now.

This History Channel was always good for a few z's, and it was playing something about dinosaurs. I tossed the half empty pizza box up onto the coffee table and lay down on the couch. The throw pillows picked out by Luisa were soft and comfortable, and I wondered how Rinaldo's youngest daughter was doing. I hadn't seen her in a while.

Not that I would go too close to her – I wasn't stupid. You didn't date the boss's daughter unless the boss told you to. He hadn't done that, though she was my age and I was considered one of Rinaldo's favorites.

Had been, anyway.

If he ever gave his blessing, I'd do her. She was hot and had a smart mouth that made me laugh. It didn't seem too likely now, not with me on the shitlist indefinitely. It was enough to make anyone paranoid, and I was already a little bit on the unstable side.

An animated T-Rex took a bite out of a Stegosaurus as my vision blurred.

Head throbbing...and the taste of dirt in my mouth. On my stomach, coughing, trying to get the dust from my lungs...but only inhaling more of it. Hands bound behind me, and I can't turn enough to the side to get my face off the ground...

I woke, startled, and glanced up at the television to see a bunch of World War II footage on the screen. I quickly shut the damn thing off. I sat up and put my head in my hands, trying to clear the memory-dream from inside.

A large wet tongue against my forearm centered me, and I reached over to scratch the base of Odin's ears.

"I need a better distraction," I muttered to myself.

Odin huffed at me as I grabbed my jacket and keys and shoved a Beretta down the back of my pants. He was probably looking at the clock and assuming I was going to work, but I'd gotten my job done earlier. Now I needed to spend some of my cash.

My parking spaces in the garage held two vehicles – a used black Mazda hatchback I had purchased on my way back from Arizona about an hour after my old Chevy truck died and a silver Audi R8 convertible that I rarely ever took out unless it was one of the high-end social occasions I sometimes felt obligated to attend.

The public transportation in Chicago was awesome, and I was a big fan of it ninety percent of the time. Every once in a while there was a need to get from one place to another door-to-door, though, and that was what I needed on this night. I slipped behind the wheel of the Mazda and headed south to the area where the gentlemen's clubs tended to spill out onto the street corners.

There were a hundred reasons I loved Chicago. Someone could live here for twenty years and still have new stuff to do. Jobs were everywhere, despite what the dudes sitting in the doorways of rundown buildings holding out cups and signs claimed. They might not have been good jobs, but there was shit to do and ways to make money. I loved the buildings the most – the whole concrete jungle idea. I loved figuring out how to get to the top of them and look down over the whole city. The Skydeck on top of the Willis Tower was an awesome place to relax.

Okay, maybe not to everyone, but I loved it.

I slowed the car as I approached the corner, and a half dozen girls and one guy took a few steps closer to the passenger side door. One of the girls actually came around to my side and laid her boobs over my windshield, smiling and grinding away at me. She was way too skinny though and had that junkie look about her. I checked the rest of them out quickly, and it didn't take me long to decide on the one with the biggest ass. My finger depressed the window button, and the guy placed his hand on the roof of the car to lean it.

"You lookin' for somethin' special tonight?"

"All-nighter," I told him. "Gimme the dark-haired girl with the round ass."

The dude leaned in a bit more, and I tilted my head a bit so he could get a good look at me.

"Yeah, I know you," he said. "One of Rinaldo's guys. Arden, right?"

"You got it."

"You sure you want that one? She's new and givin' me a bit of trouble." He snickered. "Nothing you couldn't handle. Fuck, might use you to make an example out of her, ya know? You do side jobs?"

"Yeah, sure," I said with a shrug. "She won't give me no trouble, though."

"Well, you give her a little discipline if ya need to, 'kay?"

"'Kay," I repeated. Like I was really going to fuck up a girl I was fucking. Pimps were assholes, no doubt about it.

"Employee discount!" he announced with a laugh and a wink. "Come over here, Bridgett."

The black-haired girl walked over to the side of the car, and the pimp opened the door for her. She looked up at him with a bit of concern.

"You're gonna be taking care of Mister Arden tonight," he said as he gave her a little push inside. "He's a good customer, so you be good to him."

SHAY SAVAGE

She only hesitated a moment before getting inside. Her tiny skirt rose up and gave me a view of her little black panties. She had on stupidly high heels – like they all did – which were going to look pretty good over my shoulders. She shivered, but I didn't know at first if the motion was from the temperature change or from nervousness.

I gave the pimp half the cash before I drove off with her. I'd owe him the rest when I brought her back, assuming she took care of me the way she was supposed to. I knew she would. However she ended up in this business, they all knew better than to piss off a client. Those who didn't know the rules ended up in the river or the lake.

"What's your name?" I asked. I knew what it was – the pimp had called her by her name – but I wanted her to say it.

"Bridgett," she replied quietly. She looked down at her hands on her lap and then tried to pull her skirt down a bit. I saw her hand tremble slightly before I looked back up at the road.

"I'm Evan," I told her. "Evan Arden. You haven't been doing this long."

"A while," she responded.

"You've never had anyone take you home before."

She glanced sideways at me and then shook her head.

"I'm not going to hurt you," I told her. "That ain't my thing. I'm an ass-man, though. You take it in the ass?"

She blinked rapidly a few times, and her fingers tensed around themselves.

"I have," she said quietly.

Her throat bobbed up and down, and her eyes tightened along with her jaw. She'd been hurt – I didn't have any doubt about that. Hookers often were, and I didn't think there was such a thing as one who wasn't broken in some way or another. This one was new, though – recently damaged.

I pulled the car over to the curb and turned sideways. Her whole body tensed up, and she pushed herself a little towards the door. I reached over and took her chin in my hands.

"Hey," I said. "I told you I wasn't going to hurt you, right?"

"Yeah." She nodded rapidly as her eyes widened.

"I meant that. I got lube, we'll go slow, and if you decide you don't want it, we'll stop. I can always just fuck you from behind – I'm good with that. Okay?"

She nodded again and relaxed slightly. I leaned over the console and placed my lips against hers firmly. She responded like she was on autopilot, which she probably was. After a couple of kisses, I backed away and looked her over once more as I tried to decide if she was going to be all right with this or not. She looked good, though – the right hair color, at least. Her eyes were light brown, though. I wasn't sure what her nationality might have been, but she wasn't Italian. Regardless, I really wanted to keep her. It was too much trouble to go all the way back and pick out another one.

"You okay?" I asked.

She nodded her head a few times, so I pulled back into traffic.

Bridgett was obviously new. She was young – maybe twenty or so – and definitely didn't have the demeanor of a street-hardened hooker. If I was a different kind of guy, I would have just taken her to some motel and given her the night off or whatever, but I was more pragmatic than that. If I wasn't doing her tonight, some other guy would be. Maybe he'd be a nice guy and maybe he wouldn't, but at least she wasn't going to get hurt with me.

At a red light, I looked over at her again, and my mind immediately began to catalog information. Long, soft-looking black hair – maybe Latino, but no accent, so she wasn't an illegal from Mexico or Cuba or anything like that. She was dressed in the typical whore attire – red mini skirt, thigh-high stockings, black lacy top that showed her lack of bra quite clearly. Nice, big, round nipples.

"Bridgett?" I asked quietly. It took her a moment to look from the window over to me. Bridgett wasn't her actual name, and she hadn't been going by it for very long. People responded very quickly to hearing sounds even remotely like their own names, and her delay was far too long. "You hungry or anything?"

"No, thank you," she replied. "I'm fine."

"There's a restaurant in my apartment building," I said. "We could eat first, if you want. It's a nice place – good food, maybe get you a drink or two? I know I could use one."

Come on, baby – go with me here.

"If you want to," she finally said.

Very complacent.

It was almost ten-thirty, and the full menu wasn't available after ten, but I ordered a couple of sandwiches with chips and a beer for me. I got her one of those vodka martinis that were a lot stronger than people realized. I tried to get her to relax a bit, but she kept glancing around the restaurant.

I contemplated for a moment.

"No one here cares what you're wearing," I told her.

Her eyes found mine.

"I look like a hooker," she said quietly.

No shit.

"You *are* a hooker," I said. I waved my hand towards the two servers near the bar. "They all know that. They'd know that if I

72

put you in a cocktail dress, flats, and one of those little old lady red hats, too."

"How would they know?"

I laughed.

"Because you're with me."

I managed to get her to settle down a little after that, and she did eat part of her sandwich and polish off two martinis while we talked about the weather and the Chicago Fire soccer team. Mostly I talked – she didn't seem to know shit about soccer. I finished my beer, tossed cash onto the table, and led her by the hand to the elevators. As soon as we stepped inside and the doors closed, I could feel her tension mount again, so I leaned over close to her ear.

"Not going to hurt you," I reminded her, and my lips pressed lightly against her neck, just below her ear.

Bridgett nodded slowly but still jumped a bit when the elevator went ding, signifying my floor.

I led her out into the hallway and to my apartment door. Her eyes widened a bit as Odin came up to sniff at her. He could be a little intimidating, and he didn't usually let people touch him. However, since he didn't bark much, he didn't often end up frightening anyone badly, and Bridgett was no exception. I didn't give them much of a chance to get to know each other as I grabbed two bottles of water from the kitchen counter and brought Bridgett to my bedroom.

My foot connected with the edge of the door, blocking Odin from the show as it slammed shut. I could hear him snuffle at the crack before he gave up and moved away. Placing the water bottles on the nightstand, I sat down on the edge of the king-sized bed and started to untie my boots.

"Those look like army boots," Bridgett observed. "A friend of mine went into the army. Are you in the army?"

"No," I said. Her babble amused me a little. "Ex Marine. Don't you know what *ARMY* stands for?"

"Um...no."

"Ain't Ready for the Marines Yet."

She snickered at the lame joke, which I figured was a good sign. Laughing brought people's guards down, and if she didn't relax, it was going to pretty much ruin my evening. I smiled up at her, and she returned the look before walking up to me and standing between my knees.

She placed her hands on my shoulders, and I tilted my head up to meet her lips as she bent over me. She tasted like vodka and pomegranate juice in my mouth, and she felt soft and warm in my hands. My fingers moved up to her shoulders and then back down again as our tongues moved around each other.

She pulled at the hem of my T-shirt, and we broke apart long enough for her to lift it over my head. Her hands came back to my shoulders, and she stroked her fingers down my chest.

I watched her eyes as she took me in. I was used to women looking at me in the gym or even going down the street. Even in the military, the chicks I served with favored me. Women usually liked what they saw – toned muscles, six pack abs, no scars.

Well, none on the outside.

My captain told me I intrigued them, which was why they seemed to flock to me. I was a quiet guy – a mystery for them to solve. I didn't know why girls ate that shit up, but he said they did and he was right. As soon as they figured you out – *really* figured you out – they didn't want anything to do with you.

It was part of the reason I preferred hired company.

Bridgett's soft lips molded against mine again, and her tongue played around in my mouth as her hands continued to explore most of my upper body. I got a good grip on her plump ass, pulled her into my lap and down against my waiting cock. Rubbing against her little thong panties felt good – too good. I needed something a little quicker for now.

"How about you blow me first?" I suggested as I pulled back a bit and loosened my belt. "It's been a while, and I want to be able to concentrate."

"Sure," she said.

"Take all that off first," I said with a flick of my finger towards her clothes. I flipped the buttons of my jeans open and slid them down my legs along with my boxers. "Leave the stockings and shoes, though. That's hot."

"Whatever you want," she said with a smile. Her eyes tightened a bit as she looked at my cock, and I knew what she was thinking. I wouldn't push her though, and she smiled up at me again like I didn't scare her.

She faked it all well. I hoped she'd get something out of it, too.

I sat back against the headboard, and Bridgett crawled over between my legs. My fingers ran through her hair as she leaned over and took me in her mouth. Warm and wet – just what I needed. She licked around the head first, and then tried to go down too far. She gagged a little and moved back, refusing to meet my eyes as she tried again.

"Look at me, sweetheart," I said, and she complied. "How long you been doing this?"

"I...um..."

"It's okay," I said. "Tell me."

"Since Monday."

"Shit, are you serious?"

She nodded.

"You want to stop?"

"No," she shook her head. "I gotta make a living."

I looked at her for a long time and wondered why I was even asking her. Since when did I care how much experience a hooker had? Even if she had been turning tricks less than a week, she might have already had more partners than I ever did.

"Go slow," I told her. My hand moved over her cheek, and she nodded slightly before wrapping her lips back around the head of my dick. I spread my arms out across the headboard and let her make the moves. "You don't have to take it all – just use a lot of tongue. That's it…look at me…show me how much you love my cock."

Her dark eyes stayed on mine as she sucked, licked, and ran her hand over what she couldn't get in her mouth. I didn't try to hold back, just let her work on me as my thigh muscles tightened along with my balls. The tingling sensation rose up, circled the base of my dick, and then focused through the tip of my cock as I let out a muted grunt and poured into her throat with a single thrust of my hips.

"Fuck, yeah," I muttered. My hand passed over her hair again as her throat worked to swallow it down. She moved me back and forth in her mouth a couple more times before I placed my hand on her cheek again. "You're good…come here."

I gave her one of the water bottles and watched as she drank half of it down while I got my breathing under control. Maybe the asshole pimp wasn't taking care of her like he should. That shit didn't make sense to me. Why have expensive pieces of merchandise you can sell over and over again and not take care of them?

At least this one wasn't strung out. I hated junkie hookers.

She placed the bottle back on the edge of the nightstand, and I pulled her to my chest. For a minute, I held her to me. Feeling her weight on top of me was kind of nice and made me feel warm and sleepy. Maybe I didn't need the sex as much as I needed the company.

"I'm gonna sleep a bit," I told her. "You can sleep with me if you want, or there's a TV in the other room, cable and everything. There's pizza in the fridge, too."

"I could use a little sleep," she admitted. "I don't usually get much."

"Hard to sleep during the day?"

"Yeah, it is."

I shifted around until I could pull the comforter and the sheets down enough to get our legs underneath the covers and then pulled her back to my chest again. She settled her cheek on my shoulder and closed her eyes. My fingers stroked through her smooth hair, and she blew warm breath over my skin.

Sleep came soon, and with the warmth of another body next to mine, it came without thought or dreams.

There was just no substitute for a good hooker.

###

OTHERWISE OCCUPIED, BOOK #2 IN THE EVAN ARDEN TRILOGY IS AVAILABLE NOW

FOR OTHER SHAY SAVAGE TITLES AND INFO ABOUT UPCOMING RELEASES, PLEASE VISIT WWW.SHAYSAVAGE.COM

OTHER TITLES BY SHAY SAVAGE

THE EVAN ARDEN TRILOGY

OTHERWISE OCCUPIED – EVAN ARDEN #2
UNCOCKBLOCKABLE – EVAN ARDEN #2.5
OTHERWISE UNHARMED – EVAN ARDEN #3

SURVIVING RAINE SERIES

SURVIVING RAINE – #1

ABOUT THE AUTHOR

Always looking for a storyline and characters who fall outside the norm, Shay Savage's tales have a habit of evoking some extreme emotions from fans. She prides herself on plots that are unpredictable and loves to hear it when a story doesn't take the path assumed by her readers. With a strong interest in psychology, Shay loves to delve into the dark recesses of her character's brains–and there is definitely some darkness to be found! Though the journey is often bumpy, if you can hang on long enough you won't regret the ride. You may not always like the characters or the things they do, but you'll certainly understand them.

Shay Savage lives in Ohio with her husband and two children. She's an avid soccer fan, loves vacationing near the ocean, enjoys science fiction in all forms, and absolutely adores all of the encouragement she has received from those who have enjoyed her work.

Made in the USA
Lexington, KY
27 August 2014